Saint Melissa the Mottled

For the final nineteen years of her etheric life, Saint Melissa
the Mottled resided in the Duke of Dimgreen's solitary
Wormwarp Hall, located in a darkened place of
wooded countryside, England.

Her story only began to emerge some sixty years after
her death in 1884. It is here unveiled, only in part.

This long-elusive text has been thoughtfully supplemented with appropriate images from the hand of the author.

Saint Melissa the Mottled

by EDWARD GOREY

BLOOMSBURY

NEW YORK · LONDON · NEW DELHI · SYDNEY

Published by Bloomsbury USA, New York

All papers used by Bloomsbury USA are natural, recyclable products made
from wood grown in well-managed forests. The manufacturing processes
conform to the environmental regulations of the country of origin.

Library of congress cataloging-in-publication data has been applied for.

ISBN: 978-1-60819-885-6

First U.S. Edition 2012

1 3 5 7 9 10 8 6 4 2

Book design by John Candell

Printed in China by South China Printing Company, Dongguan, Guangdong

Even now, some sixty years having elapsed since she passed, it is impermissible to speak with candour of her major subversions:

letters she wrote are still to be delivered.

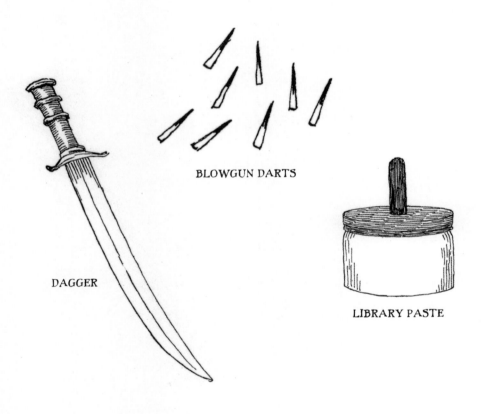

DAGGER

BLOWGUN DARTS

LIBRARY PASTE

traps she set are still to be sprung.

pronouncements she devised are still to be promulgated.

ᛋᚺᚻBBIᛏᚹ ᚱIᛋᛏ
IᚹᚹᛋI
BᚢᛏᛏR
'ᚷᛏᛏᛋᛏ
'ᛏᚷᛋ RIᚱIᛋᚷ
ᛏᚢRᚼIBᛋ
ᛏᛏᛏ
ᛋᚻᛏB

objects she hid are still to be found.

The screaming monotony of her duties at Wormwarp Hall
was, perhaps, alleviated by the machinations above hinted
at, temptations, and working of miracles.

Her supernatural triflings, of which seventy three
were at last authenticated for her canonization,
were without exception, of ruinous order.

Among them may be
mentioned: the permanent
withering, when he was
eleven years of age, of the
cricket-mad seventeenth
Duke of Dimgreen's arm;

the vile inebriation of Lady Isabel, from the quaffing
of a harmless punch of fruit juices, at a hunt ball,
and her subsequent withdrawal to the stables;

the fizzling of fireworks of magnificent intentions
on the ninetieth birthday of the Dowager Duchess;

the elopement of Ronald Sackless, a guest down
from Cambridge, with the head gardener;

and a number of peculiar collapses.

Her own collapses occurred more frequently and
grew in severity as she neared the end of her life;

in 1884 she was carried off by the vapours.

During the course of her
embalmment the true
pigmentation of her flesh
was discovered, and
attempts to redisguise her
corpse all failed.

She was interred in the Dimgreen vault,
a brass engraved with a verse of her
own creation pressing on her face.

When they went to dispose of her possessions they found, at the back of a drawer, a ribbon on which was embroidered, among lilies and forget-me-nots, the following variation on the 218th maxim of la Rochefoucauld: 'L'hypocrisie est un hommage que la vertu rend au vice.'

The nature of her life, unhappily, was such as to conceal
its events; information concerning them is as thin and
intricate as the masses of lace she left behind her.

She was born out of wedlock in 1843 at Rome. There
her mother fled, having been betrayed by the Church
of England in the person of one of its curates.

At Ostend on holiday, so she informed those who
attended her accouchement, and sank into a
delirium which lasted for weeks.

The future saint arrived, punctual and effacing, and was seen to
be blessed with the frail physique, which kept her health constantly
precarious for all of her life, and the piebald skin, blanched and
deep raspberry, which earned for her the modification of her name.

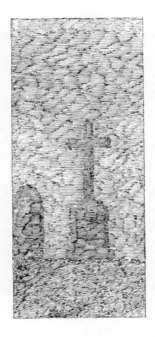

Afterwards, both mother and infant
disappeared, the latter unweaned,
the former forever.

As the sun sank on an evening at the end of summer, 1848,
Melissa, now walking, was seen by tourists to enter the Vatican.

This was the initiation of her
life's vocation as a spy; whether
foreknowledge of what she would
endure prompted the faint
screams, which so affected the tear
ducts of the ladies of the onlooking
party, is not certain. (She was later
to write, in a secret letter, of sunsets:
'... their vulgar inflammations
render me giddy ...')

For sixteen years she crept the corridors of the Papal City,
leaving them infrequently, and then always to spend a week
or two at one or another of Europe's watering places, leading
English children younger than herself down to the sea.

During these years, apart
from her sacred studies and
the systematic torture of
her sensibilities, she was
instructed in worldly arts:
the speaking of French, Italian,
and German; tatting, knitting,
crocheting, and petit-point;

the mounting and acting of seemly charades;
the bringing on of migraine;

the construction of watery poetry; the subtleties of
admiration of whisker and moustache;

painting on china; the involutions of penmanship and
calligrams; modes of address and the bending of cards;
the pressing of seaweed; the refinements of lust;

the arrangement of flowers, both living
and dried, and certain wild grasses; the
brewing of possets and tisanes.

Her ultimate months
were devoted to
the apprehension
and application of
maquillage.

In 1865 she answered, in second mourning, an advertisement for someone to accompany the two daughters of a Manchester draper home to England, their own governess incapacitated by retinal hemorrhages resulting from overly zealous peering in galleries and churches.

It was on the Channel crossing that Miss Smudge (the nom-de-guerre which had been chosen for her by a greater authority) performed her first miracle of Destruction.

She caused, while she herself was below, a gull to viciously
attack her charges as they promenaded the windy deck.

Her thoughtless disregard for her own safety, once she was summoned, in fighting off the bird, and the highest references, forged by angels and delivered to her through the flue in temporary lodgings in London, obtained for her, within a few days of disembarking, the post of governess

in the household of the Duke of Dimgreen, where
she remained entrenched until her death.

A NOTE ON THE AUTHOR

A truly prodigious and original artist, Edward
St. John Gorey (1925–2000), gave to the world over one
hundred works, including *The Gashlycrumb Tinies*,
The Doubtful Guest, and *The Wuggly Ump*; prize-
winning set and costume designs for innumerable
theater productions from Cape Cod to Broadway; and
a remarkable number of illustrations in publications
such as the *New Yorker* and the *New York Times*.
Gorey's masterful pen and ink illustrations and
his ironic, offbeat humor have brought him critical
acclaim and an avid following throughout the world.